THE CHINESE INVENT Printing

James Cunningham

CRAZY COOL CHINA

ROSEN PUBLISHING
NEW YORK

SinolinguA
华语教学出版社
BEIJING

Jointly published in 2021 by Sinolingua Co., Ltd., Beijing, China, and
The Rosen Publishing Group, Inc., New York, New York, United States.

First Edition

Editor: John Kemmerer
Cover Designer: Haley Harasymiw
Interior Layout: Rachel Rising

Photo credits: Cover, pp. 4, 8, 12, 16, 20, 24, 28, 32, 34, 36, 40, 42 ViewStock/Getty Images; p. 5 Yakobchuk Viacheslav/Shutterstock.com; p. 6 Leonello Bertolucci/Getty Images; p. 7 Chinnapong/ Shutterstock.com; p. 9 DEA/A. Dagli Orti/De Agostini Picture Library/Getty Images; p. 10 Editor at Large/ Wikimedia Commons/File:CMOC Treasures of Ancient China exhibit – Fragment of Xiping stone classics, detail.jpg/CC BY 2.5; p. 13 Sovoto/Universal Images Group/Getty Images; p. 14 User:Parhamr/ Wikimedia Commons/File:Pen ts'ao, woodblock book 1249-ce.png/PD; p. 17 British Library; p. 18 The Metropolitan Museum of Art, New York, Gift of Paul Pelliot through the Morgan Library, 1924; p. 21 Bridgeman Images; p. 22 Nicolas Asfouri/AFP/Getty Images; p. 25 © BnF, Dist. RMN-Grand Palais/Art Resource, NY; p. 26 China Photos/Getty Images; p. 29 Shelly Rivoli/Alamy Stock Photo; p. 30 Yang Liu/ Corbis Documentary/Getty Images; p. 33 Pictures from History/Bridgeman Images; p. 35 Xinhua/Alamy Stock Photo; p. 37 The Metropolitan Museum of Art, New York, Bequest of James Clark McGuire, 1930; p. 38 Ann Johansson/Corbis Historical/Getty Images; p. 41 Westend61/Getty Images; p. 43 alterfalter/ Shutterstock.com; cover and interior pages background pattern Sylfida/Shutterstock.com.

Some of the images in this book illustrate individuals who are models. The depictions do not imply actual situations or events.

Cataloging-in-Publication Data

Names: Cunningham, James.
Title: The Chinese invent printing / James Cunningham.
Description: New York : Rosen Publishing, 2022. | Series: Crazy cool China | Includes glossary and index.
Identifiers: ISBN 9781499469219 (pbk.) | ISBN 9781499469226 (library bound) | ISBN 9781499469233 (ebook)
Subjects: LCSH: China—Antiquities—Juvenile literature. | Printing—China—History—Juvenile literature. | Inventions—China—History—Juvenile literature.
Classification: LCC Z186.C5 C866 2022 | DDC 070.5'930951—dc23

Manufactured in the United States of America

CPSIA Compliance Information: Batch #BSRYA22. For further information contact Rosen Publishing, New York, New York, at 1-800-237-9932.

Contents

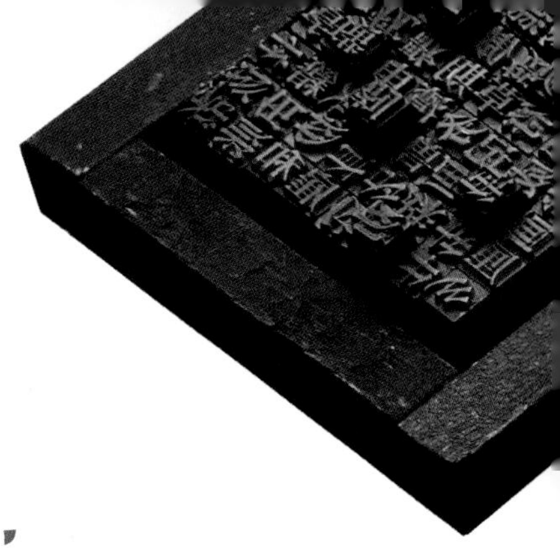

Printing:
One of the "Four Great Inventions" of China

Even though we exist in an increasingly digital world, our daily lives continue to be surrounded by and dependent upon printed material. Most of us still read physical books and magazines. Our money is still printed on cotton and linen paper. The products we buy—cereal, toothpaste, shampoo, smartphones, laptops—are contained in packages that are covered in print and include printed instructions and important information. We use printers to create physical copies of our most important documents or cherished photos.

The earliest and most basic form of printing might also be the most deeply human. Cave walls throughout Asia and Europe feature handprint **stencils** that are about 35,000 years old. These were made simply by applying **pigment** to the hand and placing the hand on the cave wall. The pigment would transfer to the stone, leaving behind an impression of the human hand.

We can now even use 3D printers to create physical objects—everything from shoes and furniture to car parts and artificial limbs.

But where was printing invented, and whom was it invented by? The answers to these questions are not simple. In large part, however, we have China to thank for the invention of printing. While simple forms of seals, stencils, and imprints began to be used by about 3,500 BCE in the Ancient Near East, printing on cloth and paper using woodblocks was first pioneered by the Chinese beginning in about 200 CE. The Chinese also were the first to use movable type of the kind that, hundreds of years later, would be adopted in Europe and lead to Johannes Gutenberg's invention of the printing press.

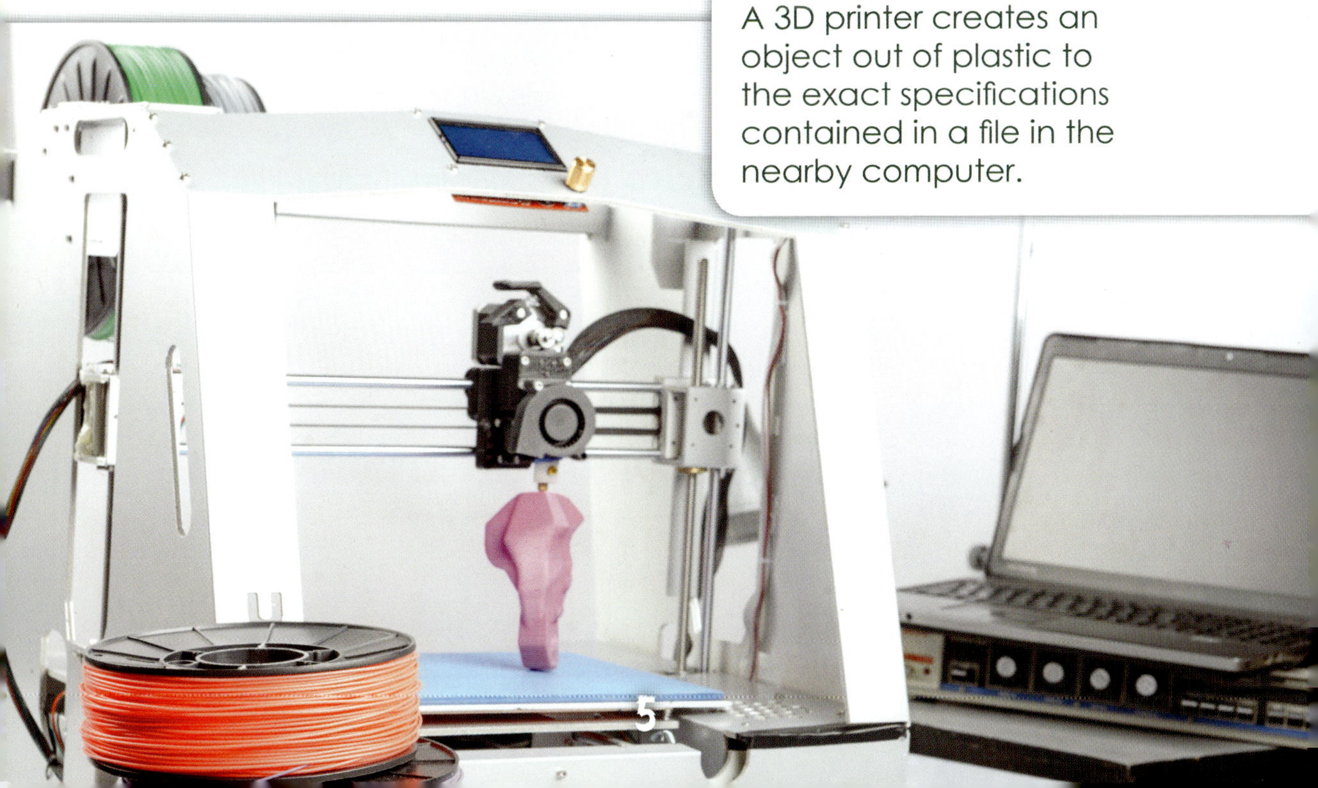

A 3D printer creates an object out of plastic to the exact specifications contained in a file in the nearby computer.

Neolithic era (10,000–4,500 BCE) human handprints appear on a cave wall in Porto Badisco, Italy. These kinds of handprints and stencils, which can be found in caves throughout Asia and Europe, are the earliest form of printing.

There is a legendary Chinese story about the invention of printing that features a man named Gong the **Sage**. Gong claimed that a **supernatural** being gave him an **enchanted** sort of jade seal that allowed him to simply blow on a piece of paper and words would magically appear. Some people think this legend is a fanciful attempt to record the invention of some kind of a printing device.

Printing is considered one of the "Four Great Inventions" of China, along with paper, gunpowder, and the compass. The paired inventions of paper and printing made knowledge affordable and available to anyone who could read, and it gave far more people the opportunity to learn how to read. Ordinary people the world over could now share in the benefits and opportunities made possible by access to education and information. Chinese innovation has given the world one of the greatest gifts imaginable—the gift of learning and **literacy**.

Widespread global literacy and easy and inexpensive access to books and printed materials are among the greatest gifts the world has received over the last thousand years, thanks in large part to China!

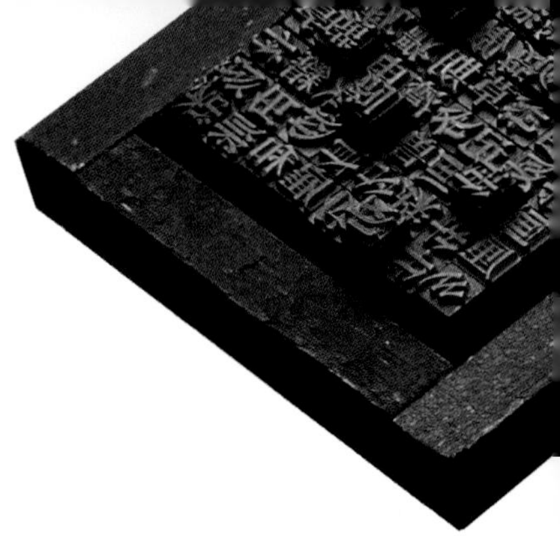

Early Forms of Printing

Simple forms of printing existed at the very dawn of written language. Beginning around 3,500 BCE, official court documents from the ancient Persian, Mesopotamian, and Egyptian civilizations were recorded in clay using cylinder seals. These seals were small, round cylinders made of a hard stone, ceramic, glass, or gemstone. They were carved with words or images or both. The cylinders would be rolled into wet clay, creating an impression. The clay dried, and a durable tablet or slab was created that preserved important information.

In some cases, seals were even used to "print" on human skin! **Taoists** used them for medicinal purposes, believing that certain characters had healing properties if pressed into the flesh of sick patients. Chinese **Buddhists** used seals in a similar way, pressing them into food to prevent disease.

Cylinder seals are a kind of impression seal. Other seals from this time period include stamp seals and finger ring seals, both of which would have been used to sign or authenticate documents. Roller stamps were also used to print images on cloth. In this case, the image wasn't carved into the stamp but appeared on raised areas of its surface. The stamp would be rolled across a piece of fabric, printing it with the stamp's decorative pattern.

A cylinder seal made of shell and bronze appears at left, while the imprint it made when rolled in wet clay appears to its right. Both artifacts were discovered at an archaeological site in present-day Tell Hariri, Syria.

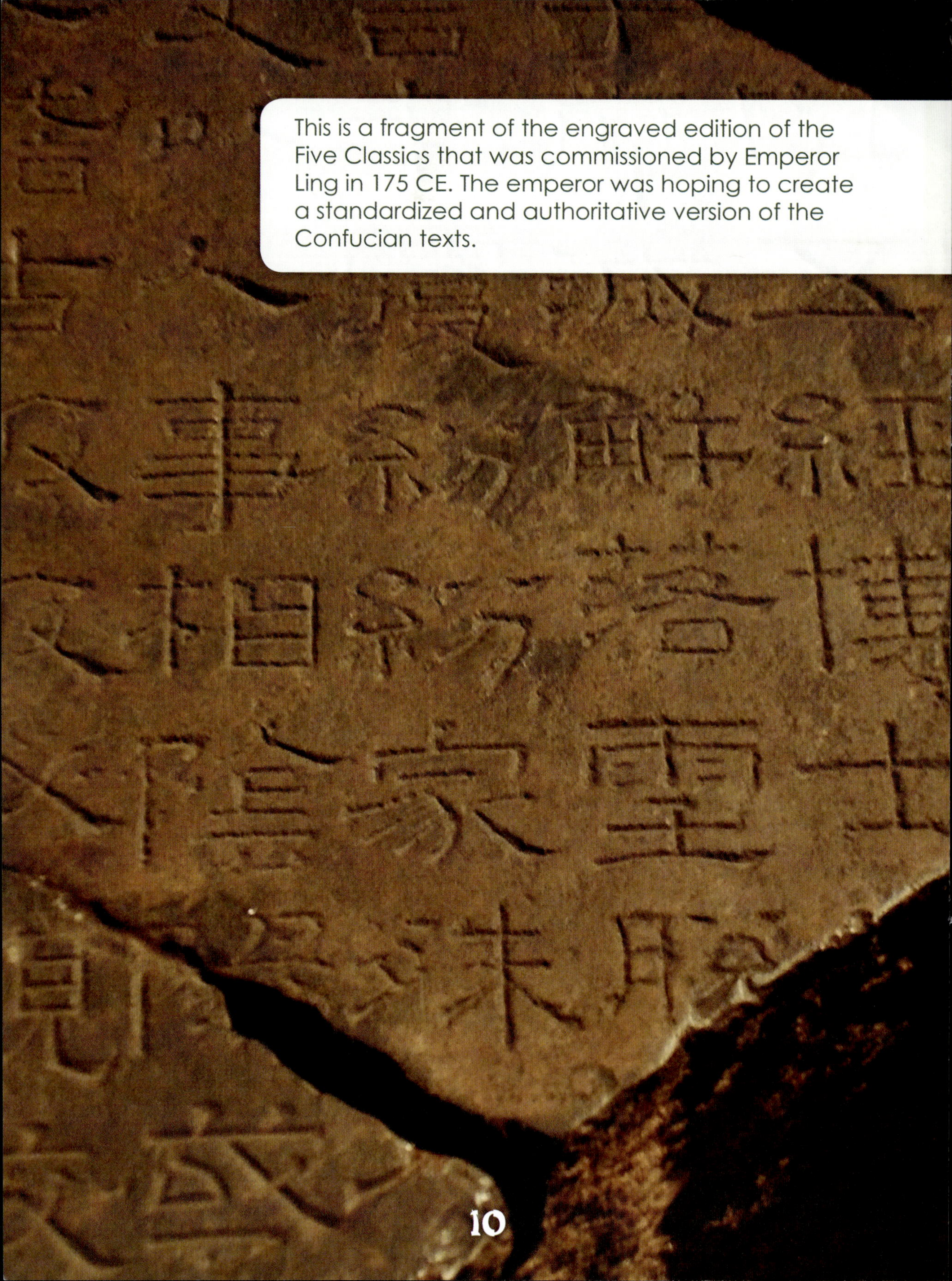

This is a fragment of the engraved edition of the Five Classics that was commissioned by Emperor Ling in 175 CE. The emperor was hoping to create a standardized and authoritative version of the Confucian texts.

In 175 CE, a Han Dynasty official named Cai Yong asked Emperor Ling to have Confucius's Five Classics engraved in stone. The emperor agreed, but there was an unexpected result. Scholars could now create cheap copies of the Confucian texts by placing paper over the carved stone and rubbing it with graphite. This was an early and very basic form of printing!

It is believed that seals were used in China beginning sometime in the Shang Dynasty (1600 BCE–1046 BCE). Early seals may have been used to create clay molds that would then be cast in bronze. They were also used to print on pottery. It was during the Qin Dynasty (221–206 BCE) that seals were first used by emperors as a signature and seal of official approval. They were usually made of stone, but wood, bone, bamboo, and ceramic were also used. The stamps could be works of art in themselves and feature **elaborate** carvings on the handle and sides. It wasn't until the Ming Dynasty (1368–1644) that seals began to be used beyond **imperial** government, as ordinary citizens began signing documents and artworks with personalized stamps. Stamps continue to be used to this day in China for government, business, and personal purposes.

Two Great Inventions Join Forces: Printing and Paper

In ancient China, a common form of preserving important information and sacred texts involved carving characters into stone or marble. With the Chinese invention of paper in the second century BCE, the carved text could now be preserved, copied, and shared widely through a very early and basic form of printing. Paper could now be laid over carved stone and rubbed with charcoal or graphite. Wherever the paper came into direct contact with the stone, it would be blackened by

Hundreds of years before they discovered how to make paper, the Chinese wrote on bone, bamboo, and even silk. All of these writing materials had obvious drawbacks. Bone provided neither a flat nor smooth surface. Bone and bamboo were both heavy, which made reading and transporting texts written on these materials a real struggle. Silk, while very light, was far too expensive to use as an "everyday" writing material.

the charcoal or graphite. But where it did not make contact with the stone—directly above the carved characters—the paper remained white. In this way, the image of the carved characters would appear in white on the blackened paper. This is the same technique people still use today to make grave or brass rubbings.

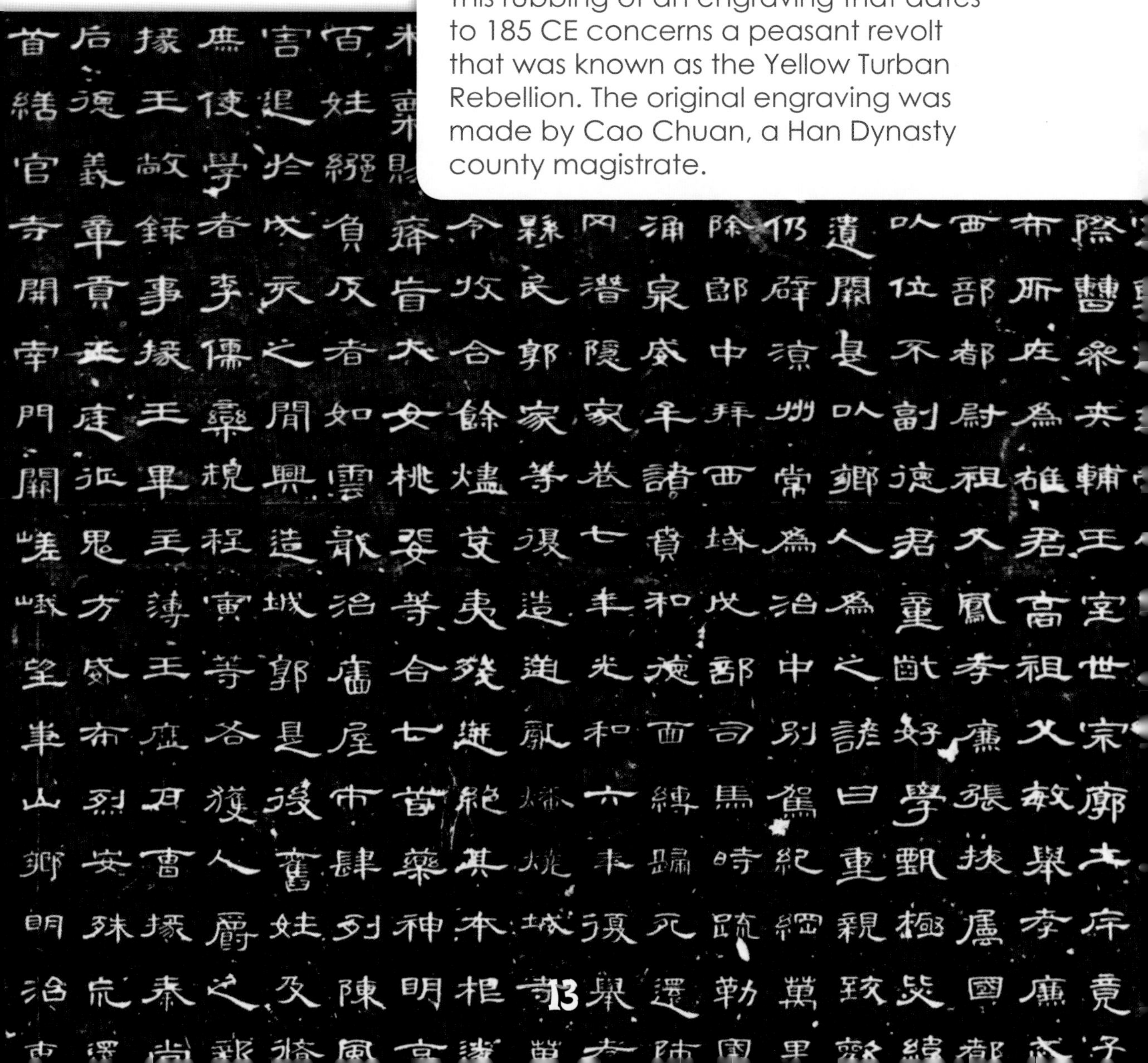

This rubbing of an engraving that dates to 185 CE concerns a peasant revolt that was known as the Yellow Turban Rebellion. The original engraving was made by Cao Chuan, a Han Dynasty county magistrate.

收蒺蔾子苗煮湯洗即立差千金翼同 **梅師方** 治難產礙胎在[illegible]并胞衣不出胎死蒺[illegible]兩爲末米湯下一匙相去四五里不下再服 **孫真人食忌** 治白癜[illegible]生擣爲[illegible] **神仙秘旨云** 服蒺蔾子一碩當七八月熟時收[illegible]後杵爲末每服二錢新汲水調下日三[illegible]數長生服之一年已後冬不寒夏不熱服之二年老[illegible]蒺蔾復少髮白復黑齒落重生服之三年身輕長生[illegible]兩等一等杜蒺蔾即今之道傍布地而生或生牆上[illegible]結芒刺此正是牆有莢者花收摘陰乾爲末每服三二錢飯後以溫酒調服治白癜風又一種白蒺蔾出同州沙苑牧馬處黃紫花作莢結子如羊內腎補腎藥今人多用風家惟用刺蒺蔾

憲州黃耆

Herbal medicine is discussed in this illustrated page from a 1249 CE medical reference book. Each page of the book was printed by an individual carved wood block.

The invention of paper is generally credited to Cai Lun, an early second century CE official in the court of the Han Dynasty. In reality, he probably improved upon the hemp paper that had been in use since the second century BCE. His exact formula is unknown, but it is thought that, in addition to hemp waste, he mixed in the bark of mulberry trees, other barks and plant fibers, shredded cloth rags, and old fishing nets.

Then, sometime around 220 CE, a better method of printing was invented. It was discovered that, rather than carve characters and images into a stone surface, it would be better for the characters and images to appear in **relief** upon a lighter wooden surface. Everything that was not a character or part of an illustration was carved away, leaving the text and images raised. Ink would be spread on these raised characters with a paintbrush, and a sheet of paper would be laid on the inked woodblock. The back of the paper sheet would be rubbed with a brush, and the ink on the block would transfer to the paper.

The result would be dark, clearly inked, and sharply defined characters and images against a high-contrast white background. Compared to charcoal rubbings, the inked text would be much more readable and the images clearer. In addition, since the wood block was reusable, copies could be made quickly and in great numbers.

Woodblock Printing

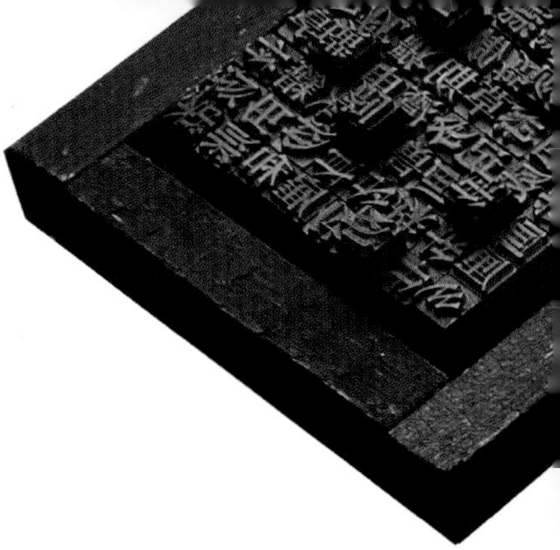

The new form of printing invented in the early third century by the Chinese became known as woodblock printing (also referred to as xylography). Despite the fact that paper-on-stone rubbings existed earlier, woodblocks are considered the world's first method of printing on paper ever developed. At first, however, woodblock printing was not associated with paper. The earliest surviving examples of Chinese woodblock printing—from about 220 CE—are images of flowers printed in three colors on silk. Words, images, and patterns could all be printed on cloth and textiles.

The Diamond **Sutra** can be dated so precisely because it contains this colophon, or printer's statement: "On the 15th day of the 4th month of the 9th year of the Xiantong reign period, [the printer] Wang Jie had this made for universal distribution on behalf of [or "in memory of"] his two parents."

It was not until the seventh century that woodblock printing on paper seems to have been developed. Buddhism and its emphasis on the spreading of **scripture**, charms, and sutras may have been the driving force behind printing on paper. Chinese Buddhists believed that sacred texts were enormously powerful as physical objects. They were thought to be able to protect against evil spirits. In addition, anyone who copied and preserved these texts hoped to receive spiritual benefits and blessings. Yet most of these printed texts were not actually meant to be read or shared widely. They were treated strictly as **ritual** objects and often buried in holy ground.

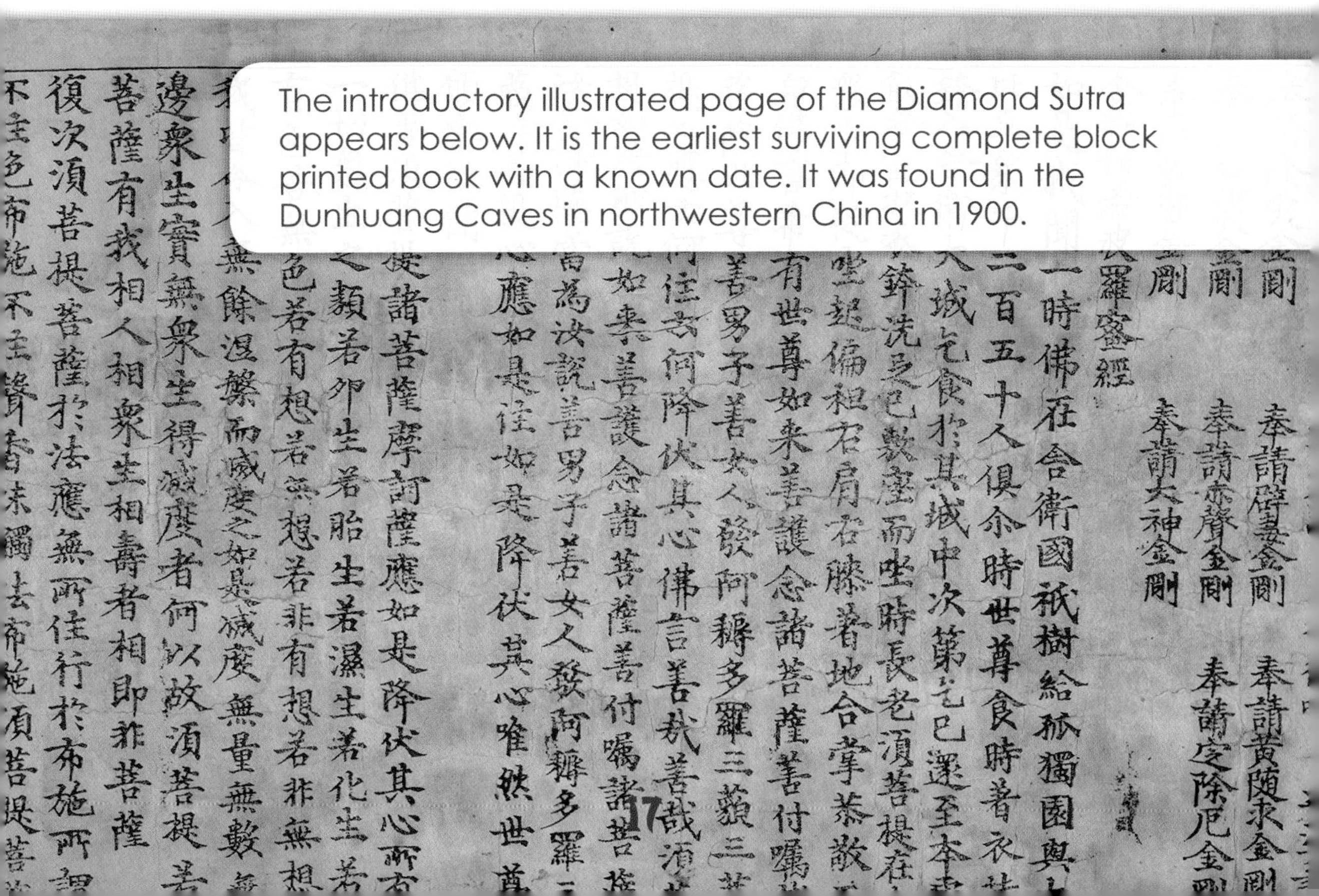

The introductory illustrated page of the Diamond Sutra appears below. It is the earliest surviving complete block printed book with a known date. It was found in the Dunhuang Caves in northwestern China in 1900.

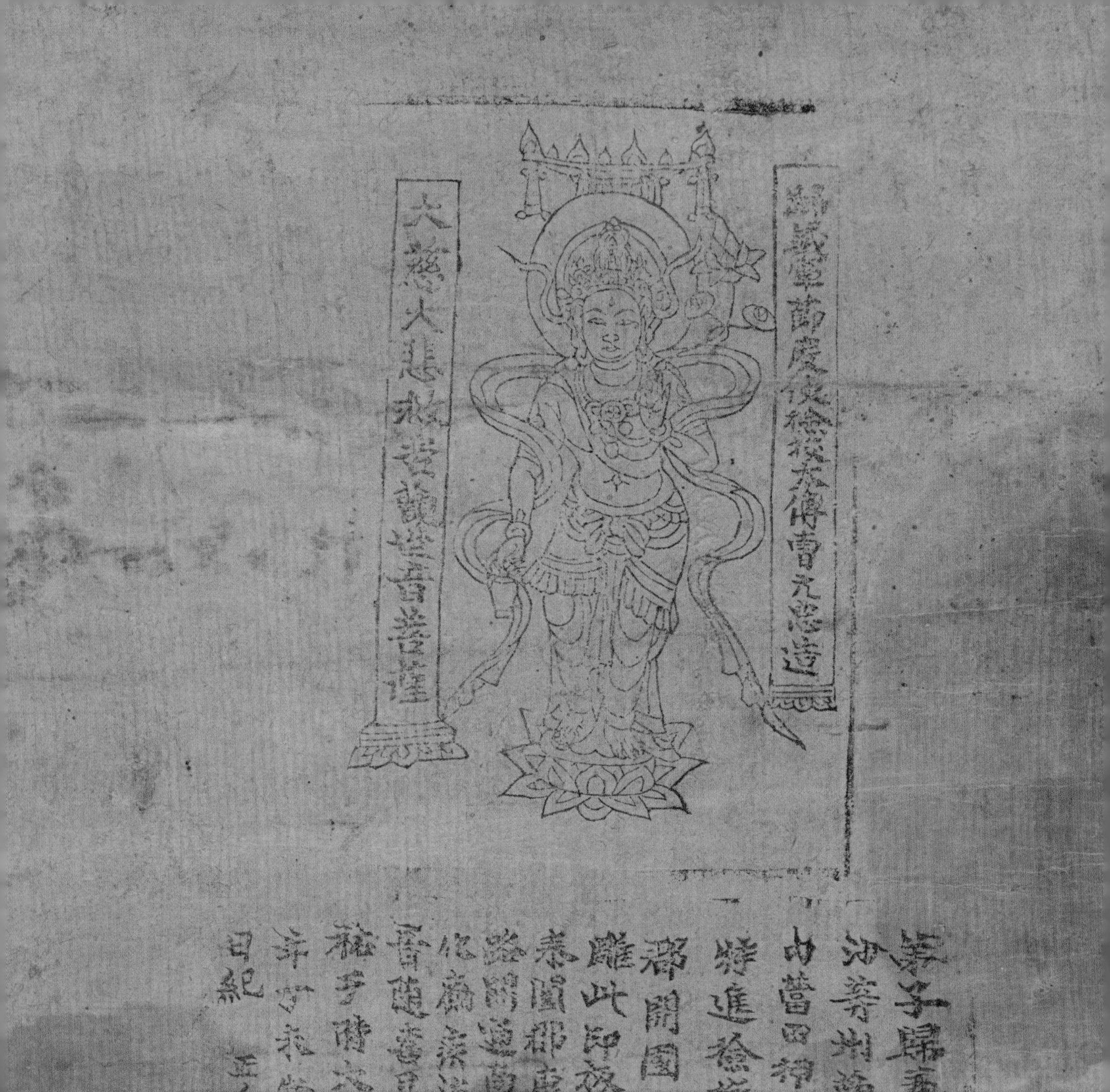

Cao Yuanzhang, tenth-century ruler of Dunhuang, commissioned this Buddhist print titled "The Greatly Merciful, Greatly Compassionate Rescuer from Suffering, Bodhisattva Guanyin." It was believed that Guanyin watched over highways, and the prayer printed here was thought to protect travelers from Dunhuang who were journeying along the Silk Road.

Following the invention of paper, most Chinese "books" were actually scrolls. The individual pieces of paper would be pasted together to form one long strip, which would then be wound around a wooden roller and attached to a thin wooden dowel. Books that took the form of a codex—paper cut and bound into pages between two covers—would begin appearing during the Tang Dynasty (618–907 CE).

The earliest woodblock print—a Buddhist chant or spell printed on hemp paper—dates to about 650–670 CE and was found in Xi'an, China. It is titled *The Great Spell of Unsullied Pure Light* and includes both text and images. One of the earliest printed texts thought to have been created to be read rather than buried or otherwise treated as a ritual object is a portion of the Lotus Sutra discovered in northwest China and dating to the end of the seventh or early eighth century. The world's oldest surviving printed book is a scroll from 868 CE that contains the text of the Diamond Sutra. The scroll is 16 feet (5 m) long and was discovered in a cave in northwestern China.

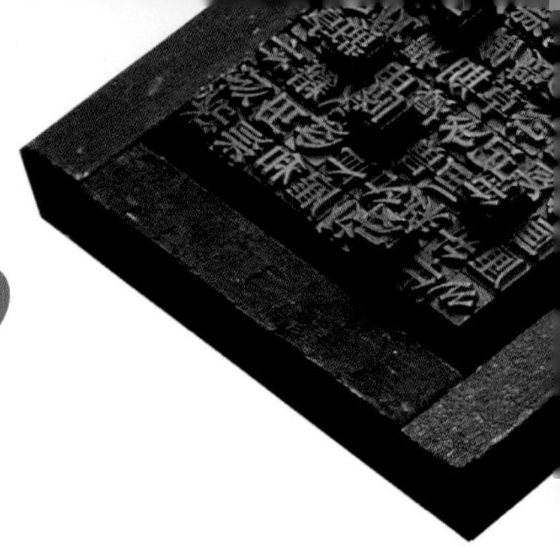

Book Production Goes Big

Beginning in the tenth century CE, book production in China began to be more ambitious. Projects were undertaken to print large multi-volume works that required tens of thousands of wood cuts and several years to produce.

Confucius ran a school that accepted students based upon their talent, rather than their wealth. He taught them his very practical ideas about family relations, good citizenship, and wise government. His students then went on to serve as advisers in the various kingdoms of China, creating a class of civil servants in China. Ever since, the civil service in China has remained open to all people of intelligence and ability, regardless of how humble their backgrounds.

The Directorate of Education during the Song Dynasty (960–1279 CE) wanted to create **authoritative** and **standardized** versions of the Confucian Classics. These are a collection of works by Confucius (551–479 BCE), the revered

Chinese philosopher, teacher, and political official. The Classics include poetry, **divination**, teachings about proper behavior and ritual observance, history, political philosophy and commentary, a dictionary, and an encyclopedia. The Classics were studied by all candidates seeking placement in the imperial **civil service** and were the basis for their examinations. The printing of the Confucian Classics stretched from 932 to 955 CE.

During this same time period, thousands of Buddhist, Taoist, and historical works were printed in scroll form. In 971 CE, the Tripitaka Buddhist **Canon**—a collection of sacred scripture—began to be printed in Chengdu, China. The entire project required over ten years and 130,000 wood blocks. Work was completed in 983, and the edition became known as the Kaibao Tripitaka.

Students sitting for a civil service exam appear in this seventeenth-century Chinese silk painting.

နိဒါနဝဂ္ဂသံယုတ်ပါဠိတော်ပါ၅၇ကျောက်ချပ်ရေး

The wood blocks used to print the *Goryeo Daejanggyeong* were destroyed by fire during the Mongol invasions of Korea in 1232. The ruler of Goryeo at the time, King Gojong, ordered a new set of wood blocks to be created and a new edition printed. It required 12 years, 81,258 wood blocks, and 6,568 volumes. This edition still survives today and is considered the most accurate of Buddhist canons written in classical Chinese.

Perhaps the most ambitious publishing project of this era, however, was one requested by Seongjong, a tenth-century ruler of the Korean kingdom of Goryeo. China's printing technology had spread to Japan and Korea beginning in the eighth century. Seongjong sent a Buddhist monk to China to request a copy of the complete Buddhist canon of scripture. The request was granted, and work began in Goryeo to print a Korean edition of the collection, which would become known as the *Goryeo Daejanggyeong*. Starting in 1011, the more than 6,000-volume work was not completed until 1087.

This Myanmar language edition of the complete Tripitaka Canon of Buddhist scripture is carved in marble and lettered in gold. The entire "book" is comprised of 729 marble slabs, each one 3.5 feet (1 m) wide, 5 feet (1.5 m) tall, and 5 inches (13 cm) thick. It is considered the world's largest book.

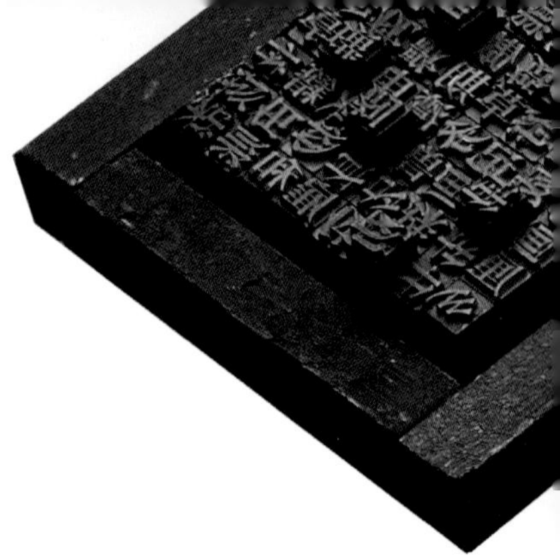

Libraries and Literacy

With the increasing use of paper for writing in the third century CE, private library collections in China began to grow. With the introduction of woodblock printing on paper beginning in the seventh century, these collections exploded in number and size.

"When I was young and devoted myself to learning, there were only one or two scholars in every hundred who possessed copies of all the classics and commentaries. There was no way to copy so many works. Today, printed editions of these works are abundant, and officials and commoners alike have them in their homes. Scholars are fortunate indeed to have been born in such an era as ours!"—Chinese scholar speaking in 1005 CE

The total number of known book collectors in China in all the centuries prior to the Song Dynasty (960–1279 CE) was only 200. By the end of the Song Dynasty, this number would more than triple, to over 700. While a large third-century private book collection might include a few hundred titles (comprised of several thousand handwritten scrolls), just 200 years later a private collector might possess 20,000–30,000 printed scrolls. By the eleventh century, private libraries typically contained thousands of individual titles and hundreds of thousands of scrolls or bound books. In addition, the Song emperors founded palace libraries, imperial libraries, and imperial academies that each possessed tens of thousands of scrolls.

Woodblock printing made it possible to produce many copies of books quickly and relatively cheaply. By some estimates, the cost of a printed book in China was about one-tenth that of a handwritten manuscript. The imperial government, commercial

Scholars read and discuss classical texts in the library of Jin Zong, a Song-era (960–1279 CE) emperor.

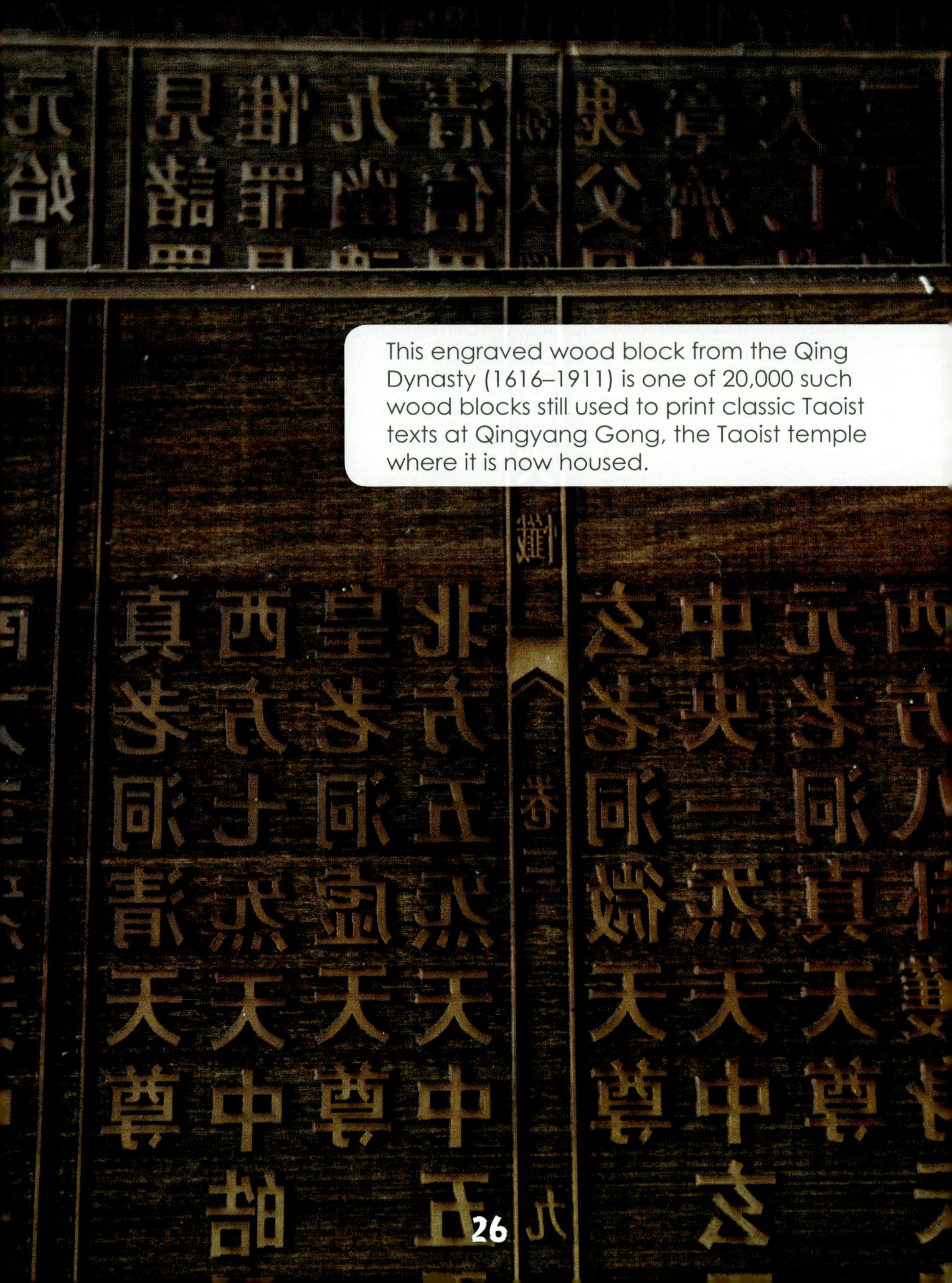

This engraved wood block from the Qing Dynasty (1616–1911) is one of 20,000 such wood blocks still used to print classic Taoist texts at Qingyang Gong, the Taoist temple where it is now housed.

"In recent years merchants engrave and print all manner of books…and produce ten thousand pages a day. With books so readily available, you would think that students' writing and scholarship would be many times better than what they were in earlier generations. Yet, to the contrary, young men and examination candidates leave their books tied shut and never look at them, preferring to amuse themselves with baseless chatter. Why is this?"—Su Shi, eleventh-century CE poet, artist, and political official

publishing companies, and private publishers all began printing encyclopedias, medical reference works, poetry, scripture, and texts relating to history and the scholarly classics. Young scholars and candidates for civil service exams could now gain easy access to the texts they needed to complete their education. In the past, these books had been very difficult to come by because they were both rare and expensive.

A larger percentage of the Chinese population learned how to read and write, thanks to this greater availability of affordable books. In 1488, a Korean official visiting China was struck by the levels of literacy found among even ordinary people. He marveled that "even village children, ferrymen, and sailors" could read.

Chinese Movable Type, Four Centuries Before Gutenberg

German inventor and publisher Johannes Gutenberg became famous for introducing movable type to Europe around 1450 CE. But what is less known is that China invented movable type hundreds of years earlier, around 1041 CE!

Bi Sheng placed his type on an iron plate that was coated with **resin**, wax, and paper ash. He would heat the plate and its sticky substances and let them cool. This fastened the type on the plate and prevented it from shifting. After printing, the plate would be reheated, which loosened the type and allowed it to be removed. The type could then be reused within an entirely different page of text.

Woodblock printing required lots of craftsman to carve hundreds of thousands of individual woodblocks to create a single book, which could take ten years or more for longer works. Those woodblocks could then never be reused except to reprint new editions of the same book, and space had to be found to store them.

An inventor and artisan named Bi Sheng (990–1051 CE) imagined a more efficient and flexible way to print text and is credited with inventing movable type. He carved individual Chinese characters into wet clay, which he then fired to dry and harden them into porcelain. He then placed the porcelain characters in the desired arrangement of text within an iron frame, forming a solid block of type. The type was coated with ink, and paper was pressed upon it firmly by brushing or rubbing, transferring the ink to its surface. When the paper was removed, the text was reproduced clearly and cleanly on the page. This was essentially the same process developed by Gutenberg four hundred years later, though he would use a mechanical press to transfer ink from the type to the paper.

The hand-carved wooden movable type in this box was used to print a family genealogy, a listing of one's ancestors and relations.

The porcelain and wooden type could be reused and rearranged to create entirely different pages of text for entirely different books. No longer did each page of text require the meticulous hand carving of an individual block of wood that could then never be changed or used in a different book.

There were drawbacks, however. The ink was thin and watery, and the porcelain type did not hold it well. The clay pieces could also bake unevenly, so the resulting porcelain type could be varying in size, creating an irregular appearance on the page.

Bi Sheng also created wooden movable type, but this, too, had its own drawbacks. The wood grain would sometimes come through in the printing process, making the letters less **legible**. In addition, when the wooden type was soaked in ink, their size and shape could change and become uneven.

Chinese movable type of the kind shown here predated Gutenberg's by 400 years. Yet, woodblock printing continued to be the most popular and efficient form of printing within China.

Metal Movable Type

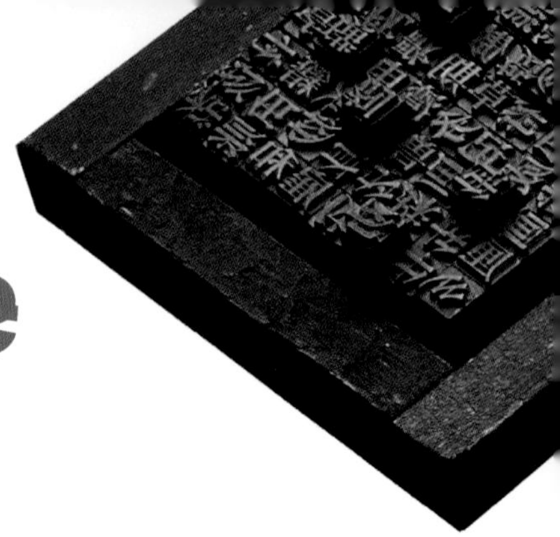

Porcelain and wooden movable type had the great advantage of being reusable, and it could be arranged and rearranged to create an infinite variety of printed text. Yet it didn't always hold ink well, and its shape and size could be irregular or become warped in the firing or inking process. The characters on the type could wear away eventually, and the type was prone to breaking after repeated use.

In China, metal type was mainly used to print banknotes (paper currency or money) and official documents. Metal type traveled to Korea, where it was adopted more widely. It was used there in 1234 to print a 50-volume book called *Prescribed Texts for Rites of the Past and Present*. No copies of this book survive. The world's oldest surviving book printed by movable metal type is an anthology of Buddhist teachings printed in Korea in 1377.

The whole process of printing created wear and tear on the type. Arranging the type, securing it onto the plate, applying pressure to transfer the ink to paper, and releasing the type from the plate all placed stress upon the relatively fragile porcelain and wood materials.

During the Song Dynasty (960–1279), Chinese printers began experimenting with type made of stronger, more durable materials. Tin movable type was tried, but it may not have held ink well. Bronze movable type was also developed with better results.

The banknote that appears on the right was printed from the metal plate at left in 1287 CE.

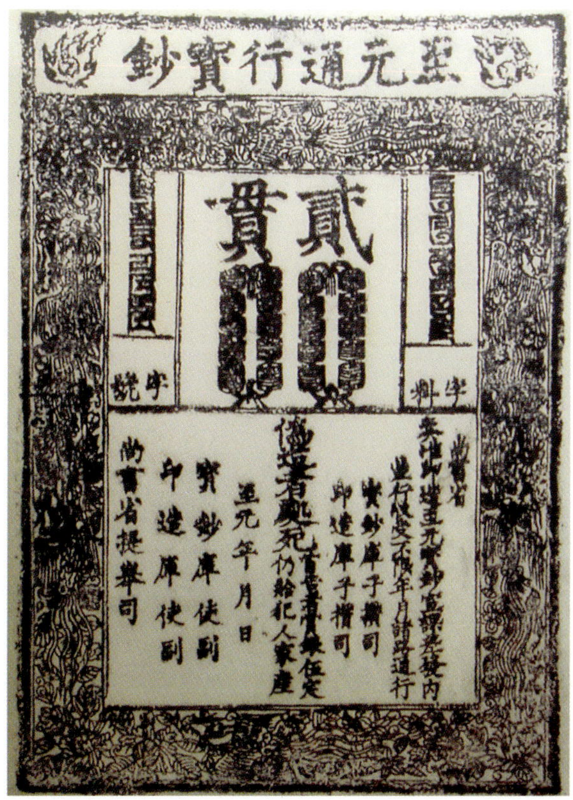

The Enduring Appeal of Woodblock Printing

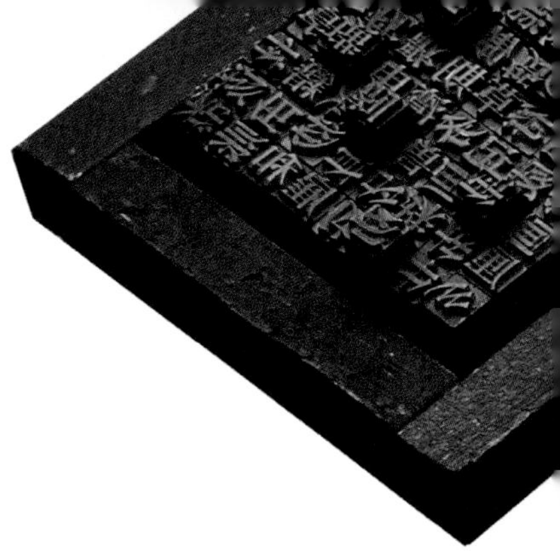

Despite the advantages offered by movable type—whether porcelain, wood, or metal—woodblock printing continued to dominate in China and throughout Asia. In fact, movable type printing was not used very much until 300 years after it was first invented by Bi Sheng. Even at the height of its popularity during the Ming (1368–1644) and Qing (1616–1911) dynasties, it is estimated that it never accounted for more than 10 percent of all printed materials. Woodblock printing continued to be the preferred method.

In 1574, the Ming Dynasty court commissioned a 1,000-volume encyclopedia that was printed with bronze movable type. The printing of a 5,040-volume encyclopedia was commissioned by Qing Dynasty emperors between 1700 and 1725. Sixty-four sets of the work were printed, making a total of 322,560 volumes and requiring 250,000 bronze movable type characters.

The reason for this lies in the large number of characters in the Chinese language. Whereas the Western alphabets derived from Latin have only about two dozen letters, there are tens of thousands of Chinese characters. Making, storing, and employing this many pieces of type was **unwieldy** and impractical. In many cases, woodblock printing was a more efficient option, and it remained the dominant printing method in China into the late nineteenth century.

A page from the Yongle Encyclopedia is shown here. The encyclopedia was commissioned by the Yongle Emperor of the Ming Dynasty in 1403 and completed in 1408. It has 11,095 volumes and about 370 million characters.

The Dawn of Printing in Europe

It is probable that knowledge of Chinese printing technology traveled the same routes that most goods, ideas, technology, and even religious beliefs traveled in the medieval era—the Silk Road. This was a network of trade routes that wound over land and sea and connected the markets and cities of Asia, the Middle East, Africa, and Europe.

Johannes Gutenberg's metal type was far more durable and uniform than woodblock lettering. The books he printed on his press were high-quality but much less expensive to make and purchase than either manuscripts or block books. This is because they could be made far more quickly, in much greater numbers, and with fewer paid laborers.

Woodblock printing on cloth began to appear in Central and South Asia and throughout the Byzantine world before the end of the first millennium CE. Woodblock printing on paper had reached Egypt by 1000 CE. Printing on cloth was common in Europe by

1300 CE, while woodblock printed paper began to appear by about 1400.

Most European woodblock printing at this time was devoted to playing cards and holy images that were sold to pilgrims. By the middle of the fifteenth century, relatively inexpensive block-books began to appear. Two of the most popular types of block-books were heavily illustrated guides to a "good" Christian death and biblical picture books (with very little or no text). However, even as block-books began to appear and become popular in Europe, woodblock printing was already being eclipsed by the emergence of metal movable type.

Woodcut religious images, like this fifteenth-century German woodblock print of St. Bridget, were very popular in medieval Europe, as were block printed playing cards.

Bible
"What we need is imagination. We have to find a new view of the world"

One of Gutenberg's first printing projects was his famous edition of the Bible in Latin, printed simultaneously on six presses in the mid-1450s. It is believed that somewhere between 160 to 180 copies were printed. Only forty-nine copies survive to this day, and they are now among the world's most valuable books.

There is much disagreement over how Johannes Gutenberg developed his printing press technology, beginning around 1439. Some historians believe the knowledge of the technology came, indirectly at least, from China. Others feel Gutenberg struck upon the idea independently of any older or existing knowledge. What is known is that his printing press revolutionized the printing industry in Europe. Movable type printing spread from Germany to Italy, France, the Netherlands, Spain, and England within 35 years. As in China hundreds of years earlier, expensive and rare manuscripts possessed by the few yielded to mass-produced, affordable books accessible to the many. Knowledge in Europe flourished, literacy increased, and civilization advanced by leaps and bounds, providing one of the most important sparks to the Renaissance.

A portrait of Johannes Gutenberg appears above a first-edition copy of his Bible, opened to one of St. Paul's New Testament epistles.

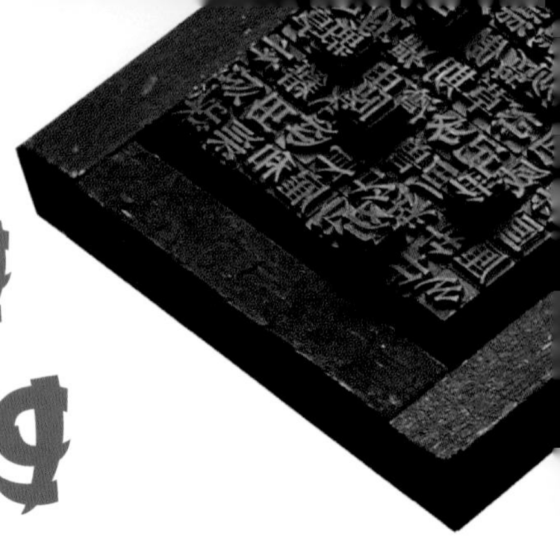

From Gutenberg to 3D Printing

Gutenberg's achievement was three-fold. He designed a mechanical printing press that applied rapid but steady downward pressure, creating a clean, crisp impress of ink on paper. He cast metal type that was much more durable and uniform than previous ceramic, wood, or bronze type. He also created oil-based ink that was longer-lasting and took to paper better than traditional water-based ink.

As revolutionary as this was, the technology of printing continued to innovate over the centuries. Advances in printing include intaglio (a kind of etching),

Using a 3D printer, amateur engineers the world over can manufacture physical objects of their own design. Models are created using 3D scanners, digital photographs, or photo-mapping software and saved to a file. The printer then builds the object layer by layer, using **polymers**, ceramic, metals, and other materials. 3D printing is not only for hobbyists. Companies have used it to build helicopter engines, jet fighter parts, and entire race cars!

color printing, screen printing (printing on textiles and clothes), and offset lithography (a photographic process used to print newspapers, magazines, books, and brochures). In the digital era, we have seen the emergence of photocopying and dot matrix, thermal, inkjet, digital, and 3D printing.

Each of these new methods has vastly expanded what we can print, how we can print it, how we can make things appear, and what we can make printers do. We have come a very long way from stamps, seals, wood blocks, and even Gutenberg's printing press!

Two technicians watch as a turbine wheel is fabricated by a 3D printer.

Celebrate China!

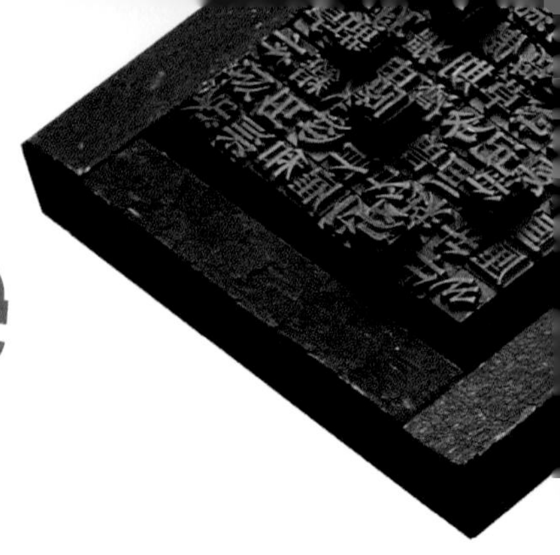

China was the first to introduce the technology of printing to the world. In doing so, China revolutionized the way information and knowledge is captured, recorded, reproduced, spread, shared, and consumed. China's invention of printing greatly increased literacy within its borders and, ultimately, throughout the world. Knowledge expanded across great distances and was available to far more people. Civilizations and societies around the world flourished as a result.

China's book industry is the world's second largest, publishing almost half a billion titles a year through more than 500 publishing houses. In addition, there are more than 8,000 periodicals published in China. Digital publishing is also growing every year, bringing in tens of billions of dollars annually.

China continues to be a world leader in the printing industry. The output of its printers is the second largest in the world. China has more than 100,000 printing companies employing more than 3 million people and generating annual revenue greater than $150 billion.

Printing is an invention that every generation finds a way to innovate and make newly relevant and useful. In one form or another, it has been around for more than 5,000 years. And, thanks in large part to China and its spirit of invention and innovation, printing is likely to remain central to human **endeavor** for another 5,000 years and beyond.

China is still at the forefront of printing technology and is one of the world leaders in book and periodical production, printing output, and revenue.

Glossary

authoritative Clearly accurate or knowledgeable.

Buddhist A follower of Buddhism, an East and Central Asian religion that is based on the teachings of Siddhartha Gautama regarding suffering and one's ability to be freed of it through wisdom, virtue, and concentration.

canon An authoritative, accepted, or authentic collection of works, including holy scripture.

civil service The administrative service of a government; the group of public servants working for a government; the bureaucracy.

divination The practice of trying to tell fortunes, predict future events, or discover hidden knowledge.

elaborate Complex, full of detail, and ornate.

enchanted Having a magical quality; placed under a magic spell.

endeavor A goal-oriented activity; a serious and determined effort.

imperial Relating to an empire or emperor.

legible Able to be read and understood.

literacy The ability to read and write; educated.

pigment A substance, such as a powder, that is mixed with a liquid and gives color to other materials.

polymer A chemical compound that is made of small molecules that are arranged in a simple repeating structure to form larger molecules.

relief Details, figures, or characters and letters that project, or stick out from, a flat surface.

resin A yellowish or brownish substance collected from the gum or sap of some trees (such as pine trees) and used in varnishes and medicine.

ritual A formal, ceremonial act or series of actions.

sage Someone known for his or her wisdom and good judgment.

scripture A collection of writings considered to be sacred and authoritative.

standardized Made to be consistent and regular.

stencil A printed pattern or text made by spraying or otherwise forcing ink, paint, or pigment though cut-out sections of an otherwise solid material.

supernatural Relating to an order of existence beyond the visible and observable universe; relating to something that seems to violate the laws of nature or is due to the actions of an invisible agent, like a ghost or spirit.

sutra A teaching from the Buddha that forms the basic texts of Buddhist scripture.

Taoist A follower of Taoism, a Chinese mystical philosophy that emphasizes following the "Way" through humility, compassion, simplicity, and living in harmony with the order of the universe.

unwieldy Not easily managed, handled, or used.

For More Information

Asia Society (three locations)
725 Park Avenue
New York, NY 10021
(212) 288-6400

1370 Southmore Boulevard
Houston, TX 77004

9 Justice Drive
Admiralty Hong Kong
852-2103-9511

Website: https://asiasociety.org
Asia Society is the leading educational organization dedicated to promoting mutual understanding and strengthening partnerships among people, leaders, and institutions of Asia and the United States in a global context.

Chinese Historical Society of America
965 Clay Street
San Francisco, CA 94108
(415) 391-1188, ext. 101
Website: https://chsa.org
The Chinese Historical Society of America is the oldest organization in the country dedicated to the interpretation, promotion, and preservation of the social, cultural and political history and contributions of the Chinese in America.

The International Printing Museum
315 West Torrance Boulevard
Carson, CA 90745
(310) 515-7166
Website: https://www.printmuseum.org
The International Printing Museum is devoted to bringing the history of books, printing, and the book arts to life for diverse audiences.

Museum of Chinese in America
215 Centre Street
New York, NY 10013
(855) 955-MOCA
Website: http://www.mocanyc.org
Founded in 1980, the Museum of Chinese in America (MOCA) is dedicated to preserving and presenting the history, heritage, culture, and diverse experiences of people of Chinese descent in the United States.

Museum of Science and Industry
5700 South Lake Shore
Chicago, IL 60637
(773) 684-1414
Website: https://www.msichicago.org
The Museum of Science and Industry is one of the largest science museums in the world and is home to more than 400,000 square feet of hands-on exhibits designed to spark scientific inquiry and creativity.

National Museum of China (NMC)
No. 16 East Chang'an Street
Dongcheng District
Beijing, China 100006
Website: http://en.chnmuseum.cn
The NMC is a palace of history and art reflecting and displaying China's traditional and modern culture. It houses more than 1.4 million objects that typify and bear witness to the richness and depth of China's 5,000-year-old civilization.

The Printing Museum
1324 West Clay Street
Houston, TX 77019
(713) 522-4652
Website: https://printingmuseum.org
The Printing Museum explores the intersections of the history, art, and technology of printing and demonstrates its enduring impact through exhibitions, interactive tours, and creative workshops. It has over 10,000 items in its permanent collection, including one of the earliest printed documents, fine-art facsimiles such as the Gutenberg Bible, and contemporary limited-edition works on paper.

Robert C. Williams Museum of Papermaking
Renewable Bioproducts Institute
Mail code 0620, Georgia Tech
Atlanta, GA 30332-0620
(404) 894-5700
Website: https://paper.gatech.edu/robert-c-williams-museum-papermaking
The Robert C. Williams Museum of Papermaking is an internationally renowned resource on the history of paper and paper technology. In addition to more than 2,000 books, the museum features a collection of over 10,000 watermarks, papers, tools, machines, and manuscripts. The museum's mission is to collect, preserve, increase, and disseminate knowledge about papermaking—past, present, and future.

For Further Reading

Bardoe, Cheryl, and the Field Museum. *China: A History*. New York, NY: Harry N. Abrams, 2019.

Basbanes, Nicholas A. *On Paper: The Everything of Its Two-Thousand-Year History*. New York, NY: Random House, 2013.

Cotterell, Arthur. *Ancient China*. New York, NY: DK Eyewitness, 2005.

Culp, Jennifer. *Ancient Chinese Technology*. New York, NY: Rosen Publishing, 2016.

Frankopan, Peter. *The Silk Roads: A New History of the World*. New York, NY: Bloomsbury Publishing, 2015.

Hanson-Harding, Brian. *Ancient Chinese Religion and Beliefs*. New York, NY: Rosen Publishing, 2016.

Harrison-Hall, Jessica. *China: A History in Objects*. London, UK: Thames & Hudson, 2018.

Houston, Keith. *The Book: A Cover-to-Cover Exploration of the Most Powerful Object of Our Time*. New York, NY: W. W. Norton & Co., 2016.

Kurlansky, Mark. *Paper: Paging Through History*. New York, NY: W. W. Norton & Co., 2017.

Liu, Jing. *Barbarians and the Birth of Chinese Identity: The Five Dynasties and Ten Kingdoms to the Yuan Dynasty (907–1368)* (Understanding China Through Comics). Berkeley, CA: Stone Bridge Press, 2017.

Liu, Jing. *Division to Unification in Imperial China: The Three Kingdoms to the Tang Dynasty (220–907)* (Understanding China Through Comics). Berkeley, CA: Stone Bridge Press, 2016.

Liu, Jing. *Foundations of Chinese Civilization: The Yellow Emperor to the Han Dynasty (2697 BCE–220 CE)* (Understanding China Through Comics). Berkeley, CA: Stone Bridge Press, 2016.

Liu, Jing. *The Making of Modern China: The Ming Dynasty to the Qing Dynasty (1368–1912)* (Understanding China Through Comics). Berkeley, CA: Stone Bridge Press, 2017.

Lusted, Marcia Amidon. *Ancient Chinese Daily Life*. New York, NY: Rosen Publishing, 2016.

Man, John. *The Gutenberg Revolution: How Printing Changed the Course of History*. London, UK: Transworld Publishers, 2010.

Melcher, Frederic G., ed. *500 Years of Printing: A Collection of Articles on the History of Printing Since the Invention of Movable Type*. Somerset, NJ: Gardner Press, 2012.

Morrow, Paula. *Ancient Chinese Culture*. New York, NY: Rosen Publishing, 2016.

Steinberg, S. H. *Five Hundred Years of Printing*. Mineola, NY: Dover Publications, 2017.

Suarez, Michael F., et al. *The Book: A Global History*. New York, NY: Oxford University Press, 2013.

Bibliography

Basbanes, Nicholas A. *On Paper: The Everything of Its Two-Thousand-Year History*. New York, NY: Random House, 2013.

Beckwith, Christopher I. *Empires of the Silk Road: A History of Central Eurasia from the Bronze Age to the Present.* Princeton, NJ: Princeton University Press, 2009.

Frankopan, Peter. *The Silk Roads: A New History of the World.* New York, NY: Bloomsbury Publishing, 2015.

Harrison-Hall, Jessica. *China: A History in Objects.* London, England: Thames & Hudson, 2018.

History.com Editors. "Printing Press." History.com. 2018. Retrieved April 2020 (https://www.history.com/topics/inventions/printing-press).

"History of Printing." History World. Undated. Retrieved April 2020 (http://www.historyworld.net/wrldhis/PlainTextHistories.asp?groupid=1951&HistoryID=ab78&gtrack=pthc).

"History of Printing." Wikipedia. 2020. Retrieved April 2020 (https://en.wikipedia.org/wiki/History_of_printing).

Man, John. *The Gutenberg Revolution: How Printing Changed the Course of History*. London, England: Transworld Publishers, 2010.

McFadden, Christopher. "The Invention and History of the Printing Press." Interesting Engineering. 2018. Retrieved April 2020 (https://interestingengineering.com/the-invention-and-history-of-the-printing-press).

Melcher, Frederic G., ed. *500 Years of Printing: A Collection of Articles on the History of Printing Since the Invention of Movable Type*. Somerset, NJ: Gardner Press, 2012.

Mote, Frederick W. I*mperial China: 900-1800.* Cambridge, MA: Harvard University Press, 1999.

"Movable Type." Wikipedia. 2020. Retrieved April 2020 (https://en.wikipedia.org/wiki/Movable_type).

Palermo, Elizabeth. "Who Invented the Printing Press?" Live Science. 2014. Retrieved April 2020 (https://www.livescience.com/43639-who-invented-the-printing-press.html).

Ropp, Paul S. *China in World History*. New York, NY: Oxford University Press, 2010.

Steinberg, S. H. *Five Hundred Years of Printing*. Mineola, NY: Dover Publications, 2017.

Suarez, Michael F., et al. T*he Book: A Global History*. New York, NY: Oxford University Press, 2013.

Tsien, Tsuen-hsuin. *Written on Bamboo and Silk: The Beginnings of Chinese Books and Inscriptions.* Chicago, IL: University of Chicago Press, 2013.

Tsien, Tsuen-hsuin, and Joseph Needham. *Science and Civilization in China: Volume 5, Chemistry and Chemical Technology, Part 1, Paper and Printing.* Cambridge, England: Cambridge University Press, 1985.

"Woodblock Printing." Wikipedia. 2020. Retrieved April 2020 (https://en.wikipedia.org/wiki/Woodblock_printing).

Wu, K.T. "The Chinese Book: Its Evolution and Development." China Heritage Quarterly. 2009. Retrieved March 2020 (http://www.chinaheritagequarterly.org/tien-hsia.php?searchterm=020_chinese_book.inc&issue=020).

Index